Table of Contents

Gold Fever
Skagway
and
Soapy Smith

by Michael R. Dougherty

That Darn Newspaper Headline

The large words printed on the page had screamed at Ed Williams so loud he couldn't ignore them. He couldn't look away. They had grabbed at his mind like a mythical Greek Siren's wail and pulled him in. There it was in the 1897 edition of the Seattle Post-Intelligencer newspaper.

"GOLD! GOLD! GOLD! GOLD! Sixty-Eight Rich Men on the Steamer Portland. STACKS OF YELLOW METAL!

Ed Williams had read it over and over. Those words had reached in and captured his very being. Was it really true? He wanted to know more. He had to know more. The newspaper story spelled out how two steam ships had arrived from the Klondike Gold Rush. The steam ship Excelsior had docked in San Francisco and the SS Portland had docked in Seattle. Between the two ships, they had carried three tons of gold from the Klondike in Canada.

"Three tons?" Ed thought to himself in astonishment. It sounded fantastic. Was gold everywhere in this far off place he'd never heard of before, called the Klondike? Was it really there for the taking? Could someone like Ed, actually go there, reach down and pick it up of the ground? Pick up gold? That darn headline.

Ed Williams was caught up in the wonder of it all. Him and thousands more. Gold Fever had him, like nothing before in his life. It held him fast in it's merciless grip. The strike was on and thousands would heed the call of Gold Fever. Would he?

Ed Williams was a young, single fellow who worked as a livery-stable keeper. He liked animals well enough, but he knew two things. He wasn't going to get rich in his job and he would probably never have another opportunity like this one in the Klondike.

Later, Ed found out that there was a place called Skagway, Alaska. It was one of the cheapest routes to the Klondike gold fields. The other was Dyea. So in an incredible burst of raw optimism, Ed decided Skagway was where he needed to go. From Skagway, he would make his way to the gold. Why not? It all sounded simple enough. Like something he could do. Something he should do. And Ed had convinced himself that it was something he had to do.

So nearly blinded by Gold Fever, Ed Williams packed up and headed for Seattle and a steam ship that would carry him to Skagway.

He wasted no time, and soon found himself on the busy Seattle docks where it seemed as if the whole world had shown up at the same time. And all of them suffering from Gold Fever just like Ed Williams. The crowd pushed and shoved their way on board anything that could float and take them north.

Ticket in hand, it was finally Ed's turn to board. He was suddenly crammed on to a steam ship with a boat load of other "stampeders" who were headed north to stake their claim. From the deck of the ship, Ed squeezed himself between two other men who were standing at the ship's railing to wave goodbye to Seattle. As Ed stood there, packed in like a sardine, looking back at the dock, his mind raced.

What would the voyage be like? Would it take days, or would bad weather delay his arrival in Skagway for weeks? And what would he find in Skagway?

With a blast of noise from it's horn, the steam ship cast off.

Ed Williams was suddenly filled with intense excitement and sheer terror at the same time. In the pit of his stomach Ed discovered a nagging feeling that this was the biggest mistake of his life. Then for one panicky moment, he nearly jumped overboard. He could have done it. Ed could have swam back to shore and forgotten all about the piercing cry of the Greek Siren's wail, that beckoned him to cast his fears to the wind and join her on the journey of his life. Ed could have jumped ship. But he didn't.

That darn headline burned in his Gold Fever brain. "GOLD! GOLD! GOLD! GOLD! Sixty-Eight Rich Men on the Steamer Portland. STACKS OF YELLOW METAL!" There was no turning back now.

A Cheechako in Skagway

Dark clouds, strong wind and heavy rain welcomed Ed to Skagway, Alaska.

His voyage on the steam ship had been a rough one. Most of the passengers, including Ed, had been sea sick the entire week. High waves and bad weather had battered the ship. And it had seemed as though the steamer would never stop being tossed into the air, then slammed back hard into the water as the ship rolled from side-to-side. Except for still being sea sick and the wind and rain greeting him as the ship entered Skagway Bay, Ed was happy this voyage had come to an end.

As he strained to see his destination while he hung on to the railing, Ed recalled an onboard conversation with a fellow passenger who had been to Skagway before. He had told Ed that the name "Skagway" was a Tlingit native Alaskan word meaning "Rough seas in the Taiya Inlet caused by strong north winds."

As the steamer finally dropped anchor in the choppy waters of the bay, Ed thought to himself that Skagway was living up to it's name. As he looked out over the settlement from the deck of the steamer, Ed notice a few rough looking buildings and a lot of tents and half buildings with tent roofs. It was a place populated with a crush of people. Ed was soon told that a small skiff boat would be used to transport passengers from the steamer to the waiting Skagway dock.

When it was finally his turn to climb off the steam ship and into the waiting skiff, Ed was soaking wet from the rain as he discover a new challenge. The steamer was bobbing up and down on the waves while the skiff was bobbing in the opposite direction. Just getting from the steam ship and into the skiff without falling overboard was going to be tricky. All this up and down motion made Ed's sea sickness worse.

Somehow he managed, although barely, to make it from the ship to the skiff without falling overboard. One poor soul wasn't as lucky and had to be fished out of Skagway Bay by both crew and passengers. As they drug the man out of the water and into the skiff, Ed chuckled to himself. He was soaked to the bone. So even if he fell into the bay, as wet as he was, he couldn't get any wetter.

When the skiff was finally full of passengers for this trip, the boat was pushed off from the steam ship. It was a rough ride in the choppy water of the bay to the waiting dock. But the moment Ed set foot on that wooden dock, his mind and body had a disagreement. Ed knew he was back on something solid, but his body felt like the waves were still tossing the steamship up and down, side to side. Time was the only thing that would help.

As he took in a deep breath of crisp Alaskan air, Ed manage to start walking forward through the crowded dock toward the beach.

As he step off the dock, his still shaky legs sank half way to his knee caps in soggy, cold mud. With each labored step, his cold, soaking wet and still sea sick body was at least getting closer to the town of Skagway. Whipped by wind and rain, Ed kept saying to himself, "don't fall in the mud. don't fall in the mud."

Everywhere Ed looked, it was like a bizarre carnival. People, animals and wagons full of goods, slogged through the mud in all directions. The crush of humanity in this small place was down right scary. But Ed hadn't seen anything yet. The wind and the rain conspired and pushed him to walk closer to a couple of buildings in search of a board walk where he could get out of the mud. But the only thing he saw was a few muddy planks here and there. Even so, there was no room to walk on them.

The sound of loud, out of tune piano music, laughter and talk filled the air as Ed slogged past the Salty Dog Saloon. Suddenly, the front door of the saloon burst open and a man with a bloody face was thrown out by two huge men. Slosh! The man fell face first in the mud, right in front of Ed as one of the huge men snarled at the bleeding man, "And stay out!" Ed quickly noticed that no one on the muddy street had even stopped to look. Everyone just kept trudging through the mud as if nothing had happened. Ed thought about trying to help the man, but he didn't because he might have lost his own sea sick balance and ended up in the mud right beside the poor man.

A little farther up the street a small noisy crowd had gathered. Curious, Ed pushed his way forward to see what was happening.

A great big, grizzled looking man was giving a terrible beating to a much smaller and terrified looking fellow. The smaller man was lying in the street, covered from head to toe with mud as the big man bent down and picked up the little guy by his neck and his in-seem. The grizzled miner then lifted the little fellow high over his head and flung him under a horse drawn wagon.

The horses spooked, reared up and began stomping and kicking in all directions. The little guy struggled to crawl through the mud under the wagon to get away from the horses and the big miner. To the delight of the gathered crowd, the mud covered little man somehow got up and slogged through the mud as he stumbled to run away. The crowd laughed as the big man growled at the little fellow, "You better run. You, you cheechako!" Then the laughter quickly died down and the crowd started breaking up.

Ed stood there a moment in the mud, the wind and the soaking rain and thought to himself, "What kind of place was this and how am I ever going to make it here?"

As Ed started to slog up the street again, he recalled a fellow passenger on the steam ship who had been to Skagway before. He had said that new comers to Alaska were called "cheechakos" and the people who have been there a while are called "sourdoughs". According to him, cheechakos were a sort of low-life in Skagway. There was even a scam aimed at them. When a cheechako bought something in Skagway, the store keepers wouldn't give them any change, no matter how much they had coming.

And if the cheechako said anything about it, they would get physically thrown out of where ever they were. On the other hand, Sourdoughs weren't cheated that way.

As Ed looked around, his still half sea sick mind remembered the gold fields and his reason for being here. And that was enough to keep him going. At least for now. Cold to the bone, soaking wet and tired of the mud, Ed spotted a place called Clancy's Saloon where he figured he could at least get out of the wind and rain for a while. Maybe it even had a warm fire for his weary, wet body.

What was in store for him in Skagway and the gold fields? Ed was too tired to care right now. But if he knew, he'd probably just turn around and go back home.

Go Ahead, Punch Me in the Nose

Drenched, tired of slogging through the mud and still feeling sea sick, Ed was ready to take refuge in Clancy's Saloon. To get there, he had to make his way across the crowded, muddy street. But half way across, he nearly fell over a large tree stump that had been left sticking up out of the mud. Ed managed to get around the stump, but then he had another obstacle. He had to step over a large log. Both were in the middle of the street right in front of his destination.

Moments later Ed pushed open the door of Clancy's Saloon. Smoke from a wood stove and cheap cigars filled the crowded room. This place had been thrown together fast to take advantage of the Gold Rush stampeders. It was dim, shabby and plenty rough. Ed managed to squeeze himself between a couple of men at the bar. They both gave him a quick look and sized him up as a cheechako.

The bartender was Clancy himself. He was red headed and Irish through and through with a temper to match. Ed motioned for a whiskey. A few moments later, Clancy slammed a glass down in front of him and sloppily filled it from a whiskey bottle. Ed quickly laid down his money. Clancy took it and moved on without a word. And just like his fellow stream ship passenger had told him, cheechakos didn't get any change. But Ed knew what he'd get if he complained about it. Ed forgot about his change as two loud drunks, just a few feet down the bar, got his attention as they argued. Clancy also kept an eye on them.

A drunk named Jackson snarled "You're just a dumb cheechako" to a new comer named LeRoy, whose slurred back with a drunken, "What in thunder's a cheechako?" LeRoy's question caused Jackson to wheeze out a laugh, down another shot of the cheap, green whiskey served in these parts and holler, "Bar keep, hit us again!" Clancy brought a bottle, filled their glasses and stayed close.

Then Jackson tried to tell a much too drunk LeRoy, "cheechakos don't know squat. They're new to Alaska. I bet you just got off the boat." To which LeRoy spit out his proud reply, "I came in last night on the Utopia Steamer." Pleased with his sharp eye, Jackson proudly and drunkenly slurred back, "I can spot a cheechako a mile away." Unfazed, LeRoy shot back with, "Well I still say, the White Pass is the fastest way to the Gold fields." Annoyed, Jackson scowled, "The White Pass is for sissies. Real men climb the Chilkoot you dumb cheechako!" But LeRoy wouldn't shut up and fired back with "You wouldn't know a real man if he walked up and punched you right in your big, fat nose."

Too drunk to care, Jackson defiantly said, "Yeah? Well give it your best shot cheechako." And with that, Jackson motioned toward the end of his nose as the target. A determined look crossed LeRoy's drunken face. He made a sloppy, drunken fist and threw a punch that somehow managed to hit it's target. The punch jolted Jackson's head backward. Wounded, he grabbed his now bloodied beak as he leaned over the bar.

Clancy had enough from these two. He grabbed his sawed off Irish Walking Stick from behind the bar and swiftly delivered it's gnarled top to the head of LeRoy the cheechako, who quickly crumbled to the dirty floor. The saloon crowd ignored the scuffle.

Then Ed noticed as Jackson lifted his head off the bar, turned to look down at the floor, then bent over LeRoy's unconscious form and quickly began going through the man's pockets as he looked for money. He found some. Then Jackson stood back up, leaned over the bar toward Clancy and secretly passed him the take.

Clancy held the money below the bar, counted it, then passed Jackson his share. Unhappy with his crummy take, Jackson checked his throbbing, bloody nose and complained in a drunken voice to Clancy. "I should be getting the 60 percent. It's my face they're punching." Clancy pushed in closer, and menacingly shoved the business end of his walking stick in Jackson's face. "It's me own saloon and by the way, me own Shillelagh that's been saving your worthless hide. You'll take 40 percent and like it, or you'll be leaving the same way he is."

With that, Clancy waved and shouted for his bouncer. A knuckle dragging gorilla of a man appeared at the bar. Jackson was afraid of him. Clancy ordered, "Be throwing that one out into the street" as he pointed to LeRoy, who was still sprawled out and unconscious on the floor.

The bouncer grunted as he bent down, grabbed LeRoy by the collar and started dragging his bones across the floor. As he did, he brutishly shoved other men out of the way.

Back at the bar, Clancy glared at Jackson, then walked away to go back to tending bar. Jackson finished his whiskey, checked his battered nose, then defiantly drained Leroy's whiskey glass before staggering off. It was becoming clear to Ed that he'd better wise up quick or he'd end up like the guy the bouncer had drug out of the bar and flung out into the muddy street.

Bare Knuckles

An ominous warning rang in Ed Williams ears.

"Watch out for Jefferson Randolph "Soapy" Smith and his men." That was what a fella had told Ed over pancakes and coffee that morning. Soapy had gotten his nickname from an unusual con he was known for. The con involved selling bars of bath soap for a dollar each to unsuspecting cheechakos who thought they had a chance to find a ten dollar bill, a twenty and even a fifty, tucked inside several of the soap bar wrappers. But what the cheechakos didn't know, was that the only ones who ever found the money were men who had been planted in the crowd by Soapy to get the suckers excited. After Soapy gave his spiel, and when the cheechakos saw that one of the men in the crowd had found money in a soap wrapper, they were more than ready to lay down their money for a chance to hit pay dirt.

Ed had also been told that in Skagway, Soapy and his thugs and con men, strong-arm cheechakos and sourdoughs alike. They also forced protection money from most of the saloons, sporting girls and other businesses. And not just in Skagway. Soapy had men on the steam ships that were coming up to Skagway so they could find out who had money. Then once they were back in Skagway, they would pass the information along so the "mark" could be set-up as a target for a later con or mugging. They even hit the trails to the gold fields. No one was safe anywhere.

Ed knew he had better keep his eyes peeled and his ears sharp or he'd get fleeced for sure. But that morning, Ed had read a poster in town that declared a "Bare Knuckles fight to the finish" in Sylvester Hall that evening. Ed was headed there. He was told to just follow the crowd.

Ed figured, he might even wager a few dollars to maybe win some more money to buy supplies so he could get started for the gold fields. He had no trouble finding Sylvester Hall. There was a good sized crowd and they were ready for action.

Inside, Ed discovered the noisy Hall was packed. Standing room only. A boxing ring had been set up in the middle of the room. Money was changing hands at a fever pace and there was plenty of beer and whiskey.

Ed looked over the room and spotted a man with a dark beard wearing a dark hat and coat. The man matched the description he was given that morning of Soapy Smith. Ed watched the man for a while and soon decided, "yep, that's gotta be Soapy Smith". With Soapy were some of his con men and enforcers. "Reverend" John Bowers, "Doc" Jackson, George Wilder and the "Sheeny Kid" who was busy shadow boxing. Close to Soapy was a mountain of a cigar chewing man. His name was Ed Burns and he was one of Soapy's body guards. But the biggest brute in the place was standing even closer to Soapy. He was Yeah Mow Hopkins, Soapys personal body guard. Yeah Mow was a veteran of the San Francisco China Town Tong Wars. No one ever fooled with him.

Soapy and his men were taking bets of their own, as Soapy shouted "gentlemen, there's plenty of money for all bets. Now who thinks the

Kilkenny Wildcat can take my boy, the Platteville Terror?" Somehow over the noise, Ed heard the ringside bell and the crowd began to settle. Then the referee entered the ring amid cat calls and boos from the rough horde.

The referee shouted, "Ladies and gentlemen, tonight we present a no holds barred, bare knucks fight to the finish."

The crowd went crazy, yelling and screaming. The rabble was hungry for action. The referee waved for the crowd to settle down then began his spiel. "And now, introducing this evening's pugilists. From Colorado, wearing black trunks. The one, the only, Platteville Terror!" The Terror ran down an isle toward the ring. The crowd cheered, booed and threw things at the boxer as he climbed into the ring and energetically bounced up and down with his arms raised high in the air.

The referee signaled the crowd to settle down once again as he shouted, "And his opponent, all the way from County Cork in Ireland, wearing green trunks, the one, the only, Kilkenny Wildcat!" A perfect villain, the snarling Wildcat defiantly made his way slowly toward the ring as he bared his teeth at the rabble. The crowd booed and hissed at the lumbering oaf.

A drunken miner spit on the Wildcat. Furious, the Wildcat attacked the drunk with a flurry of hammer-like punches. The crowd loved it and screamed for more. To oblige, the Wildcat delivered a punch that knocked the drunken miner out cold. Several men grabbed hold of the miner's limp body and dragged him out of the Hall. The Wildcat continued his defiant stroll toward the ring. Some in the crowd hurled objects at him. The Wildcat gave them a show by snarling and clawing at the air in their direction.

Moments later in the ring, the Wildcat played up his villainous roll to the hilt. He strutted around the ring, showed his teeth, snarled at the crowd and punched at the air with claw-like hands. The crowd hated him. He loved it and so did they.

A bell signaled that the fight was on. The two fighters sprang into action. Fists flew. The noise of the throng was deafening. As the fight raged on, Reverend Bowers leaned in to talk with Soapy. "Brother Jefferson, we have a lot of cash riding on the Terror. Are you certain he's going to win?" Soapy took a slow drag off his cigar, exhaled the smoke and said "the Wildcat hates anything Scottish, so I have a little surprise in store for him."

The Wildcat attacked the Terror, he delivered a series of hard punches, and knocked him against the ropes. Ed watched as the two fighters went into a clinch and the Wildcat viciously bit the Terror on the shoulder. The Terror screamed in pain. Blood poured from his shoulder. The Terror looked at his bloody wound and the Wildcat threw a couple of hard blows at his off-guard opponent. The crowd was in a frenzy over the cowardly foul-play. The Wildcat continued his assault as he punched both the Terror's ears at the same time. The bell sounded the end of round one. True to form, before he went to his corner, the Wildcat kicked the Terror square in the groin. The Terror crumbled to the floor. One hand was on his ear and the other was on his aching inseam. Most of the rabble screamed foul again. But some cheered, because they were loving every gruesome second of the savage display. More bets were placed and Ed manage to place his bet on the underdog.

Round after round the exhausted and bloodied fighters kept trading punches. Then Soapy leaned over to Ed Burns, and Burns got up and pushed his way to the back of the screaming crush.

In the ring, the Wildcat appeared to be going in for the kill. He threw a flurry of tired, labored punches at the Terror. The Terror tried to cover his face and headed for the ropes. The crowd booed the Terror. As he enjoyed his assumed victory, the Wildcat followed the Terror to the ropes and mustered his strength for a final brutal assault. The crowd was in a total frenzy. The Sheeny Kid was shadow boxing himself into a stupor. Reverend Bowers cringed, put his hands together and looked toward the Heavens in prayer. Even Soapy looked a little worried. Then it happened.

The sound of loud Bag Pipes suddenly filled Sylvester Hall. Curious and confused, the crowd looked around for the source of the unusual sound. And there, in the back of the Hall was cigar chewing Ed Burns. He was smiling like mad and standing next to a red-haired man in a Scottish Kilt, who was playing the bag pipes. The Wildcat heard the sound and stopped beating on the Terror. As he snarled and looked for the source of the sound, the Wildcat paced the ring like a crazed animal. He screamed in anger. "I'll kill him. I'll kill him. Where is that slimy, Scottish dog?" Then with the Wildcat away from him, the Terror came alive and bolted off the ropes toward his angry opponent who was paying no attention to him. The Terror hit the Wildcat with a hard one that sent him spinning. The crowd roared. The crazier the fight, the better they liked it. Not giving up, the Terror gave the Wildcat a relentless beating. Then, the Terror delivered a brain-jarring blow to the Wildcat, sending him to the floor with a sickening thud. The crowd became totally silent.

The only noise in the hall was the strange sound of air as it escaped from the bag pipes and the labored breathing of the exhausted fighters. Quickly, the referee stood over the Wildcat and began his count. "One, two, three"... The crowd watched intently as the referee continued. "Four, five". The Wildcat struggled to get up. "Six, seven". The Wildcat somehow managed to get up on one knee. The silent crowd was tense and waited to see if... As the referee continued his count, the Wildcat fell back to the floor. "Eight, nine" hollered the referee.

The Wildcat again struggled to get back up. He tried with all his might but only managed to lift his head. Then one last snarl and his head slammed back to the floor. He was out cold. The referee hollered "ten!" Then turned to the Terror and grabbed the boxer's arm. He then raised it high in the air and shouted, "The winner by a knock-out in the twenty-sixth round. The Platteville Terror!" The crowd went completely insane. The terror's trainer jumped into the ring as the Terror collapsed. The Wildcat's manager began trying to revive his uncooperative fighter. Sylvester Hall was filled with celebration as the Scottish Bagpipe again filled the air with victorious music.

Ed Williams could hardly believe what he had just seen. That was a bizzare fight. But Ed had even made some money and things were looking up. Tomorrow, he would start getting things in order so he could head for the gold fields in a few more days.

But Soapy's men had other plans for Ed.

He Should Have Known Better

It was late morning as Ed made his way through the still muddy street to the Skagway Information Center. Last night after the bare knuckles fight, while Ed was collecting his winnings, he talked with a man about his plan to head out for the gold fields as soon as possible. The man had told him that he had just come back from the gold country. The man had gone on to tell Ed that he should go to the Skagway Information Center where they could give him important information before he headed out. It had sounded like a good idea.

With his winnings from the bare knuckles match, Ed figured it was time to get started on his trip. A tiny bell rang as Ed open the front door of the Skagway Information Center where he made his way into the sparsely furnished, Spartan looking office. Ed was greeted cheerfully by a man who stood behind a counter at the far wall. There was no one else in the office. The man asked Ed if he was planning to strike it rich in the gold fields. Ed found himself getting excited about his upcoming adventure and to learn what kind of information the man had that would help him get started.

The happy fellow asked Ed, "which pass you figurin' on taking to get to the gold country?" Ed had no idea. So the man offered him some free information. "The Chilkoots the fastest, but it's a mighty steep climb and you might have to hire some help to carry your outfit." He continued with, "The White Pass isn't nearly as steep and you can use horses to haul your gear. But it's a longer trail and you won't be gettin to the gold as quick."

As the man talked, the tiny bell rang again and a rotund man with a toothless grin and moon-face came in and stood behind Ed.

As he thought it over, Ed still didn't know which pass to take, then the man behind the counter said, "I have maps of each pass. They even show you where the poison springs are located." Ed hadn't heard anything about poison springs before. This was getting hard.

The man behind the counter continued. "You accidentally drink from one of them poison springs and you can forget about ever reaching the gold fields. You'll be dead in an hour." It was looking harder and harder to get to that gold. Then the man smiled, and said, "I'm glad you stopped by today. My maps of the passes could save your life. Just get one for each pass, look them over and you can decide which way you want to take to the gold country. The maps are a dollar each and a bargain at that." Ed was sold. He needed the maps.

Excited, Ed quickly reached into his coat pocket, pulled out a healthy roll of money and started to take out two dollars. Suddenly, the moon-faced man behind Ed snatched Ed's money and violently slammed his huge body up against Eds. The force of the blow smashed Ed's ribs into the edge of the hard wood counter. Ed cried out in pain as the moon-faced man ran to the door, jerked it open and vanished into the crowded muddy street. The tiny bell rang again as it signaled the man's escape.

With a shocked look on his face, the man behind the counter asked, "Are you alright?" Ed clutched his painful side. Then the kind man behind the counter asked, "Did he get your money?" Ed suddenly realized what had just happened. He'd been robbed. "Yeah, he got everything but my winnings from last night." Then, in an almost knee-jerk reaction, Ed bolted out of the office as he held his screaming ribs.

Out on the street, Ed spun around, and looked up and down the crowded street as fast as he could. He almost made himself dizzy. But there had been no sign of the moon-faced man. Ed clutched his painful side and thought that he might have a broken rib or two. Most of his bank roll had been stolen. He was angry at the thief and himself for letting it happen. Ed decided to head down the muddy street to see if he could find the Marshal's Office.

After a while, Ed had just about given up. His ribs were really hurting. Then, as he glanced up the way, he spotted it. A small sign read "Marshal" and Ed headed toward it. As Ed opened the door, he spotted a man sitting at a desk. Almost afraid to ask, he said, "You the Marshal?"

The man behind the desk looked up at Ed sternly and answered, "Marshal Rowan. What can I do for you?" Happy to have some help at last, Ed started with, "I just got robbed in the Skagway Information Center." Marshal Rowan quickly looked irritated and exasperated as he shook his head and shot back with, "You dumb Cheechakos will never learn. You ever heard of Soapy Smith?" His words gave Ed a sinking feeling in the pit of his stomach as he gave a disgusted replied. "Yeah, I heard of him."

Marshal Rowan continued with, "The Skagway Information Center is one of Soapy Smith's fronts." That was it. Ed had heard enough. He felt really low right at that moment when he realized that he had walked right into one of Smith's places and just let it happen. But he wanted his money back and asked. "Then if you know who stole my money, can you get it back for me?" Marshal Rowan let go a laugh. "I've shut down the Skagway Information Center before. But it just keeps coming back." Then Rowan leaned back in his chair. "Skagway is a rough town. I got more trouble here than you can imagine and I'm just one man. I don't even have a deputy." Ed tried once more as he asked, "What about my money?" Marshal Rowan shook his head no, "Can't help you. There's nothing I can do. Good day." Ed grabbed his aching ribs and grimaced. As Rowan noticed he asked, "You OK?" Then Ed chuckled to himself in defeat. The Marshal was right. Skagway was a rough town. All Ed could say was, "No I aint." Then Ed turned slowly and walked back out the door and onto the crowded street.

What was he doing here?

The Swamper

His cracked ribs throbbed, and Ed felt lost as he walked aimlessly through town. And what Marshal Rowan had told him about not being able to help him get his money back, was ring in his ears.

"Yeah", he said to himself, "Welcome to Skagway you dumb Cheechako." Up ahead was a wood plank building. Ed had decided he would just lean up against the side of the structure and think things over for a spell. "What am I doing here?" he asked himself out loud. As he watched the crush of people who were going here and there, the answer came to him. "You're here for the gold. Ok, so you were robbed. Are you just going to fold up like some Cheechako fresh off the boat? Or are you going to make it happen? If others can make their way to the gold fields, then why not you?" As Ed stood there, almost pleased with himself, he had forgotten about the pain from his aching ribs. Money. He needed money to replace what had been stolen. Then he remembered Clancy's Saloon. Maybe Clancy had a job he could do to earn some money.

With a renewed strength, Ed headed over to Clancy's to see if he'd give a Cheechako a break. He took a deep breath for courage as he walked into Clancy's Saloon for a second time.

It was just as crowded, noisy and smoky as it was before when Ed had first gone in a couple of days ago. Ed made his way across the crowded floor and walked up to the bar like he owned the place. Before he realized it, the words "I'll have a whiskey" loudly flew out of his mouth. Clancy was behind the bar and he brought over a bottle, a glass and poured his drink. Ed put his money on the bar, and said, "Clancy, do you need any help? I'm looking for work." Clancy picked up Ed's money and stopped as he gave Ed the once over. "You really lookin' for work?" asked Clancy. Ed was glad he had at least caught his attention.

Ed shot back with, "I sure am." Then Clancy paused a brief moment before he said, "Will you be knowin' what a swamper is?" Ed thought a moment then answered, "Can't say as I do." Clancy pressed on sternly with, "Swampers clean up in the bar and that includes the spittoons. It's lousy work. But if yer serious, come back tonight, you'll work from 10:00 at night until well after closing when you'll be putin' the chairs up on the tables and moppin' up the floor."

It sounded like lousy work, but he need a job. So Ed replied, "I'll take it." Then Clancy said, "Good. I'll be seein' ya back here at 10 sharp." Clancy started to leave, then turned back, leaned in close to Ed and said, "What ever money you'll be findin' on the floor is yours to keep. I don't pay swampers. And I get 10 percent of what you find. And by the way, if I catch you cheatin me, you'll be getting the business end of my Shillelagh walking stick over your head." And with that, Clancy went back to filling drink orders.

Well, at least Ed had a job. He quickly began asking himself how much he was going to make as he picked up money that had been dropped on the floor? A moment ago he'd never even heard of a swamper. Was this his ticket to the gold fields?

Later that night, Ed was back at Clancy's just before 10 and let Clancy know he was there. Clancy hollered for someone to show him where they kept the mop, buckets and rags. The next thing he knew, Ed was cleaning up after a fight between two miners. Later, he saw a strange game that was being played by a few grizzled men who had just got back to town from the gold fields.

One of the men took a flaming log out of the wood burning stove with his bare hands, as he laughed and tossed the smoldering wood to one of the other men, who quickly tossed the hot log to another, who tossed it to yet another. The grizzled men were drunk and laughed as they tossed the hot log, back and forth, back and forth. Then, one of the men fumbled when he burnt his fingers on the log as he tried to catch it. The burning log crashed to the floor. The one who had just dropped the burning log had to buy a round of drinks for the others who had been playing the crazy rough house game.

As for the money, Ed had noticed how much was being dropped on the floor during the night. When he reached down to pick it up, he had to ignore what the money had been laying in. Ed had also been careful to make sure none of the customers saw him picking up the money. Likely as not, they would have been willing to fight him for it, no matter how dirty it was. Being there all night, Ed had started to get used to the loud noise that constantly filled the saloon. Later, in the early hours of the morning, Clancy closed up and his bouncer shoved out a few stragglers. After that, in the quiet of the empty saloon, Ed had noticed that his ears had begun to ring from the noise of the night.

Ed went to work and cleaned up the huge mess. While he cleaned out the spittoons, a really disgusting job, Ed found coins in the bottom of one of the containers. He cleaned them off and then stuffed them in his pocket. All together, he had made decent money on his first night. And he had remembered to set aside 10 percent of his take for Clancy.

Trouble at the Golden Mule

Early the next morning it was quiet in Skagway, but not for long.

Nursing a hangover, Andy Magrath, a well known prospector, headed for a drink of whiskey at the Golden Mule Saloon. Inside the dingy establishment, John Faye, a smelly, overweight slob, was taking chairs off the tables in the empty saloon, preparing for another day. Magrath make his way in. His hang over had him in a bad mood as he asked, "You open?" Faye was his usual bad-tempered self as he shot back, "Ya, I'm open." Magrath snarled, "Then gimme a whiskey and make it the good stuff."

Faye shuffled behind the bar and grudgingly set up Magrath with a shot of the good stuff. With that, Andy put his money on the bar. Fay grabbed the money, put it in the till and started drying glasses. Magrath knocked back his drink, savored the expected affect, then realized he didn't get his change. "Barkeep. Where's my change?" Faye didn't bother to look up. He just kept drying a glass as he asked, "What change?" Magrath's head hurt too much as he shot back, "I got change comin'. Where is it?" Faye stopped working on the glass and looked up at Magrath as he said, "You ain't gettin' no change." Magrath wasn't about to get cheated as he snarled, "Whaddya mean? That change scam's for Cheechakos. I ain't no dumb Cheechako.

Defiant, Faye held firm with, "I don't care what you are Magrath. I said no change." Magrath had enough. "How bout I get the Marshal over here?"

Then Andy Magrath slamed down his empty glass and stormed out of the saloon into the crisp morning air.

A few minutes later, Magrath burst through the front door of Marshal Rowan's office. Marshal Rowan was sipping coffee at his desk and startled as Magrath hollered, "I'm sick of the scum that's taken over this town and I want you to do something about it now." Rowan furrowed his brow as he shot back with, "What are you talking about?" Magrath sputtered, "That pig barkeep over at the Golden Mule owes me change and won't pay up."

The Marshal was nearly out of patients as he snapped back. "Change? Magrath are you drunk or just plain stupid? I got better things to do than settle some petty beef over change."

Determined, Magrath sternly shot back, "Well if you won't do something about it, I'll go back over there and beat it out of him." With that, Magrath quickly started for the door. As he did, Rowan slammed his hands down on the desk and shouted, "Hold it Magrath."

Andy Magrath stopped and turned back toward the Marshal who continued with, "Alright... alright, I'll go over there. At least we can settle this peaceful-like."

Back in the Golden Mule Saloon, Faye was standing behind the bar, sweating and shaking as he looked nervously toward the front window and waited. Then Faye spotted Magrath and Marshal Rowan headed his way. Faye put his nervous, sweaty hands around a double barrel shotgun that he kept behind the bar. He slowly cocked both barrels.

Marshal Rowan and Magrath charged into the saloon as Magrath shouted, "Now I'll git my change." Quickly, Faye swung the shotgun above the bar and fired both barrels. The blast shattered the quiet morning. Andy Magrath flew back hard, and hit the wall dead. His body slumped to the floor. Marshal Rowan was blown through the front window, and out into the street in a hail of broken glass.

Faye was breathing heavily, and shaking violently. His hands still clutched the murder weapon. His eye's riveted on his victims.

The Mob

A loud commotion outside woke Ed up with a jolt. His was tired and bleary-eyed from working into the early hours of the morning. Ed rubbed his eyes, checked his watch and discovered that he'd only had a few hours of sleep. But there was something going on out there.

Once outside Ed learned that John Faye, the owner of the Golden Mule Saloon, had just shot and killed a miner named Andy Magrath and severely wounded Marshal Rowan. Ed followed the crowd to the Golden Mule, but he held back. Not getting too close, but close enough to see what was going on.

An angry, noisy mob had formed. They hollered and shouted that they wanted to hang Faye. A terrified Faye struggled as some men drug him out of the Golden Mule Saloon and onto the street. A rope choked his neck as he gasped for air. His hands had been tied behind his back. The mob had gotten bigger and louder. Suddenly, the sound of a rifle shot rang out and the crowd became quiet as they looked around.

Soapy Smith and his men had shown up with rifles. Then Soapy stepped forward and shouted at the crowd, "What do you men think your doing?" An Irishman named Murphy spoke up in a loud voice, "We're about to hang this murderin' scum, what's it to ya?" The mob shouted in agreement and some raised their arms and pumped their fists in the air. Then Soapy fired his rifle toward the sky and shouted, "What's your reason?" But Murphy wouldn't let it go as he yelled back, "Faye killed

Andy Magrath and shot up Marshal Rowan. How's that for a reason?" The mob exploded in agreement again. They shoved, pushed and Faye was knocked down into the muddy street.

Again, Soapy fired his rifle. This time it was aimed over the heads of the mob. Then the mob became quiet as Soapy shouted, "Did anybody see him do the shooting?" Murphy reacted quickly with, "He had the gun in his hands and that's good enough for us." The blood thirsty mob shouted in agreement. But Soapy hollered out, "Then if no one saw the shooting, I say Faye deserves a fair trial." Not happy, Murphy snarled at Soapy, "Who in blazes are you to be sayin' what should be done?" The angry crowd shouted in agreement.

Soapy looked intently at the mob and sternly said, "As long as I'm in Skagway, there's not going to be any vigilante hanging. Now turn Faye over to me."

"You're not the law" shouted Murphy "And we don't have to listen to you." Nobody moved or said a word. They watched. They waited. Then Soapy cocked his rifle and lowered it at Murphy who quickly got a nervous look on his face.. Soapy's men followed his lead as they cocked their rifles and took aim at the crowd.

Silence and fear gripped the mob. As he looked right at Murphy, a steal-eyed Soapy declared, "I'm going to say this just once. Turn Faye over to me right now or we'll open fire. And I promise you Murphy, you'll be the first to die." Soapy motioned to one of his men and said, "Red, get Faye."

The mob waited tensely as Red started toward Faye. Murphy continued to look into Soapys eyes and could see that he meant business. Murphy didn't want to die. So Murphy, with his eyes still fixed on Soapy, hollered to the mob, "Let him go." The mob was angry and began shouting "No!"

As he kept his eyes fixed on Soapys eyes, Murphy quickly shouted down the mob with, "I said let him go!" The crowd quickly became silent once again.

As Red pressed into the crowd, it was so quiet that he could hear the sound of his boots as they squished through the mud with each step. Then Red stopped and bent down to help Faye up out of the muddy street. Then Red took the rope off of Faye's neck. As he did, Faye breathed hard as Red untied Faye's hands.

Murphy then pressed Soapy with, "What are you figurin' to do with Faye?" Soapy answered loudly so the entire mob could hear him. "See to it that he gets a fair trial. Now you men go about your business." But no one moved. There was only silence.

Then Soapy shouted, "I said go on, get out of here. There isn't going to be any mob hanging in Skagway." Angry and frustrated the crowd grumbled as they slowly began to break up. Murphy stood there for a moment as he continued to look at Soapy. The two men looked at each other intently. Then Murphy slowly turned and walked away. As he did, Soapy relaxed and lowered his rifle. His men did the same.

Ed Williams had been standing back a ways as he watched from next to some buildings across the street. He had heard what was said. For a moment, when Soapy and his men had rifles pointed at the crowd, Ed thought gun fire was going to leave people dead in the street. It had been a tense moment. But it wasn't over yet.

Pass the Hat

The tension in the air was so thick you could have cut it with a knife.

Soapy and his men had taken Faye down the street to "Jeff Smith's Parlor", a small bar and gambling establishment owned and run by Soapy Smith. It was Soapy's headquarters in Skagway. Earlier, Soapy had told Reverend Bowers to stay on the street, keep an eye on the mob, and to report back to him if the mob had a change of heart.

Inside Jeff Smith's Parlor, Soapys heavily armed gang was waiting when Soapy and the men who had faced the mob, returned. Back inside, Soapy pushed Faye into a chair as he snapped, "Sit down." Faye was shaking badly as he pleaded, "Don't let them hang me Mr. Smith. The other day, you told me if I did this for you, I'd be protected. You promised." Soapy shouted at Faye, "Shut up."

Suddenly, Reverend Bowers rushed into the Parlor and announced, "Brother Jefferson, Marshal Rowan just died and there is a very angry mob headed this way. This time they have two ropes." After hearing that, Faye was terrified and again pleaded for his life. Then Soapy ordered his men, "Get that front window open now and when I give the signal, I want to see a bunch of rifles pushed out through the opening and pointed right at the mob." Then, Soapy thought for a moment and said, "Now listen to what I'm about to say. Nobody fires a shot. Nobody! Any man who does will wish he was never born."

No one spoke. The only sound was Faye's sniveling. Then Soapy turned to Reverend Bowers and said, "Marshal Rowans wife is with child. The baby will be the first born in Skagway and is due any day now." With that, Soapy told Reverend Bowers to hand his bowler hat to Nate, the bartender, at Jeff Smith's Parlor. Then he told Nate to open the till and put a fist-full of money in the bowler.

Soapy turned to his men and commanded, "Every one of you reach into your pockets right now and fill up that hat." As they did so without question, Doc Jackson looked out the open window and saw the mob as they approached. He turned back to Soapy and calmly said, "Here they come." Scared half to death, Faye cried out, "No, no, no." As he Ignored Faye, Soapy looked at his men and sternly ordered, "Alright muscle-heads. Remember. No shooting."

Then Soapy looked over at Reverend Bowers, and told him, "Wait for my word, then bring that hat out full of money." The Reverend nodded his understanding. With that, Soapy turned toward the door and with rifle in hand, walked confidently out the door to greet the mob.

As he stood there on a thin board walk, Soapy watched as the crowd approached. The angry, festering mob stopped in front of the Parlor. Two men in front were carrying ropes. Murphy stepped forward to say, "Smith, we'll be wanting' Faye. And this time, if you try to stop us, you'll be hanged right along with him for standin' in the way of the law."

The mob shouted at Soapy. Soapy remained calm and hollered out, "Law... you speak of the law while you stand there ready to hang one man without a trial and another just because he stood in your way? What kind of law is that?"

Soapys words had made the crowd even more angry and they shouted at him. Then Murphy showed his resolve as he shouted back at Smith, "We're not here to argue Smith. Now be gittin' out of our way, we're taking Faye!" Then, as the crush of the mob pushed forward, Soapy gave his men the signal. Suddenly, a bunch of rifles pushed through the open window and pointed right at the surprised crowd. Fearing they would be shot, the mob became quiet and stopped dead in their tracks. Some stepped back.

Soapy hollered at the crowd with, "I've got fifty armed men in there. All I have to do is give the signal and they start shooting. And that's exactly what I'm going to do the next time one of you vigilantes takes another step forward." Murphy shouted back at Soapy. "Faye killed Andy Magrath and now Marshal Rowan is dead too. Why are you protecting scum like that?" The mob erupted in shouts of agreement.

Then an angry man in the crowd named Johnson shouted, "Marshal Rowans wife is having a baby. What about that?" Again, the crowd defiantly joined in loud agreement. But Soapy saw an opening and hollered back, "How's stringing up Faye going to help the Marshal's widow and baby?" The mob had no answer. Soapy continued with, "If you really cared, you'd be out doing something for them, instead of looking to do some murdering on your own." And with that, Soapy turned to the Parlor and called for Reverend Bowers.

The Reverend stepped out of the Parlor, with his filled bowler hat in hand. Then Soapy started back in on the crowd. "While you men have been running around looking to spill more blood, the good people of Skagway have been collecting money for the widow Rowan and her precious child."

Reverend Bowers addressed the crowd as if he were a real clergy. "Come brothers, give that the poor widow and her child shall not go hungry." And with that, the Reverend stepped off the board walk saying, "Give as we have already."

Murphy looked at the Reverend then reluctantly stuck his hand in his own pocket, and pulled out some money and stuffed it into the hat. Others in the mob started mining their pockets and putting what they could in the hat as it was passed around.

A second hat joined in the collection.

Then Major Strong, the editor of the Skaguay News came forward and spoke to Soapy. "Smith, you know me. As editor of the Skaguay News, I will be responsible for Faye's safety if you'll hand him over."

Strong continued with, "I promise he'll get a fair trial." Soapy pondered the offer for a moment, then said, "Do I have your word on it Major

Strong?" Strong nodded and offered, "Yes you have." Soapy turned back to the Parlor and commanded, "Bring out Faye."

A moment later, Ed Burns forced a terrified, wide-eyed and still shaking Faye outside. Soapy looked at Faye and said, "No harm will come to you. They promise and I promise." And with that, Soapy looked back over the crowd and said, "Gentlemen, you're doing the true and proper thing. And our town, the glorious town of Skagway will be better for it." Ed Burns stepped off the boardwalk with Faye in hand and Major Strong stepped forward to take Faye. Then Major Strong addressed Soapy. "Smith, I don't believe that you stand for what's true and proper in Skagway. But your insistence that Faye gets a fair trial is the right thing to do." And with that, Major Strong and a few others took Faye off to jail.

As they watched the crowd move away, Reverend Bowers quietly told Soapy, "That was mighty close Brother Jefferson." Soapy gave Bowers a shrewd smile as he continued keeping one eye on the crowd as it broke up. Then Soapy offered, "Our plan worked. It strengthened our hold on this town and Marshal Rowan is no longer a problem. And Faye wouldn't dare talk." As Soapy looked back at Reverend Bowers he continued with, "But I think we're going to have to deal with Major Strong and his newspaper. He's a crusader, a do-gooder. And he has the printed page as his own personal forum... He is most certainly our enemy."

Things had been rougher than usual that morning. While Ed Williams had felt relief that there was no hanging, the town had been shaken as the forces of good and evil continued to do battle in this place called Skagway.

As Ed headed back to his bunk to try and get a little more sleep, he thought about what he had witnessed and what the rest of the day might bring. Ed also felt good because he had been able to put some money in one of the hats that had been passed around. Before Ed continued on to his waiting bunk, he stopped and looked out at Skagway Bay. How many Cheechakos, bitten by Gold Fever, would get off the next steamer? One thing was sure. If any of them wanted to head out for the gold country, they needed to want it bad enough to survive Skagway.

The skinny pillow that waited for Ed in his bunk was sure going to feel good.

It Was a Set-Up

He had nearly frozen to death up in the Klondike last winter. But he had kept at it. Then one cold, snowy day he plunged his pickax into the frozen bank of a creek and something caught his weary eyes. He had reached down and picked it up. There, in his trembling, half frozen hand, had been a small bit of gold. His name was J.D. Stewart and his strike had kept him in the Klondike all winter and spring until his claim had played out and there was no more color to be found. He was fresh from the gold fields when he arrived in Skagway. Stewart had figured to celebrate the pouch full of gold he had managed to coax out of the bank of that creek as he happily made his way into Jeff Smith's Parlor.

As he entered triumphantly, Stewart shouted across the room to Nate Pollock the bartender. "Set me up with a shot of whiskey barkeep. I'm just down from Dawson to celebrate my strike."

Then before Stewart had his first drink, two men who had been sitting at a near-by table, Clyde Fogle and Moose Johnson, invited Stewart to join them. A happy Stewart agreed and strutted over to their table. Then, after his first drink, the two offered to buy him another. Stewart said, "That's mighty kind of you." To that, Moose Johnson said, "Our pleasure mister. We both prospected in the fields. We know what it's like to half kill yourself for a smidgen of gold dust." Proud of his strike, J.D. Stewart was quick to tell them that he found more than a smidgen of gold and that his poke was full. The three drank to Stewart's good fortune and continued drinking for some time. J.D. Stewart got drunk, while Fogle and Johnson had been careful not to. Something was up and while he didn't know it, J.D. Stewart was about to turn Skagway upside down.

The Eagle Was In On It

Ed Williams had never seen the streets of Skagway filled with the kind of talk he had been hearing.

There was an anger in the air that was so thick you could have cut it with a knife. Ed learned that something had happened to a fellow named J.D. Stewart earlier in the day. And that a man named Clyde Fogel and another man known as Moose Johnson had gotten J.D. Stewart drunk in Jeff Smith's Parlor. Then the two had taken Stewart out back to see a scraggly old stuffed eagle attached to a pole in the fenced back yard of the Parlor. Once outside, the two men had invited Stewart to step up for a closer look at the eagle. When he did, Fogel and Johnson had hit him over the head from behind, which knocked Stewart out cold. Then the two men had robbed him of his gold-filled poke before they escaped through a secret trap door in the fence. When Stewart had come to, he had a terrible headache and there was no sign of Fogel or Johnson. Moments later, Stewart panicked when he discovered his poke had been stolen.

Drunk, addled by the blow to his head and plenty angry, J.D. Stewart had stumbled back into Jeff Smith's Parlor to let the bartender know that the two men he'd been drinking with had stolen his poke in the back yard. But the bartender, Nate Pollock, only snarled at Stewart and said, "You're drunk mister. Go on, get out." But even in his drunken state, Stewart realized it had all been a set-up. The barkeep, the two men, the free drinks. Even the stuffed eagle had been part of the con.

So Stewart had left to go to the office of the new Skagway lawman, Marshal Taylor who had replaced the murdered Marshal Rowan. But what J.D. Stewart hadn't known was that Marshal Taylor was already on Soapy Smith's payroll. Taylor refused to help Stewart. Determined, J.D. Stewart had shouted at Marshall Taylor, "Then I'll get someone else to help."

He didn't know who to turn to, so Stewart had headed for the office of the local newspaper, the Skaguay News. There he told his story to the editor, Major Strong.

After he heard J.D. Stewart's story, Major Strong headed out to find a man named Frank Reid, a surveyor who had laid out the town of Skagway. Reid was a known adversary of Soapy Smith. After Strong told Reid what happened to Stewart, the two agreed that it was past time for justice to be served in Skagway. They decided to get the new Commissioner to step in and order Soapy Smith to give back J.D. Stewart's poke full of gold. The two knew that Soapy wouldn't like that at all.

A Storm Is Brewing

Between puffs, Soapy nervously rolled a cigar between his fingers.

He stood at his bar in Jeff Smiths Parlor. Except for Soapy and his men, the Parlor was empty. Suddenly. The Sheeny Kid burst in, and quickly walked over to Soapy as he stammered, "Word on the street is... that... uh... Frank Reid got the new commissioner and their gunna tell you to be giving back that Stewart fellow's gold." As he heard the news, Soapy turned to his body guard Ed Burns and demanded, "Ed, I want you to find Clyde Fogel and Moose Johnson. And when you finish with them, I'm going to personally kick their butts onto the next boat headed for Seattle." Ed Burns was quick to reply, "Right boss" as he headed out to find the two men. As Ed left, Soapy said to no one in particular, "Gentlemen, unless I miss my guess, this night will be a very trying one for us all." Then, once again, Soapy nervously rolled his cigar. His face had an uncharacteristic worried look. A very worried look. The bar was strangely quiet. Suddenly, a voice outside the Parlor hollered out, "Smith, we want to talk to you!" Soapy recognized the voice was that of Frank Reid.

Hand It Over Or Else

A Group of men stood just outside Jeff Smith's Parlor.

The door of the Parlor opened and Soapy walked outside. After a moment, Soapy addressed the crowd with, "What can I do for you gentlemen?" The new Commissioner quickly spoke up. "Cut the bull Smith. You know why we're here." Soapy tried to remain calm as he responded courteously with, "How do you do Commissioner?" Then Frank Reid pressed Soapy. "Where is J.D. Stewart's gold?" Soapy drug out his response as he took a long drag off his cigar and slowly blew out the smoke. When he was good and ready, he answered, "Why don't you ask the men who won it from him fair and square in a card game?" Frank Reid shook his head and shot back impatiently, "Stewart didn't loose his poke in a card game. It was stolen by your men." Then the Commissioner spoke up again. "Mr. Smith, we know what happened to Stewart's gold. Now you have until eight o'clock tonight to return Stewart's property or we will take action." Before Soapy could respond, Frank Reid spoke up again with, "Thanks to some of your thugs, your luck just ran out. You have until eight tonight." And with that, the group of men turned and walked away. Soapy stood there a moment watching the group. He took another drag off his cigar, then angrily threw it into the muddy street before heading back into the Parlor.

Once inside, Soapy walked back to the bar. No one said a word. Then Reverend Bowers spoke up. "This situation seems very serious brother Jefferson." The Parlor was quiet once again as Soapy thought.

His men didn't know what to say. They stood there looking at Soapy, and waiting for him to tell them what to do. But, lost in his own thoughts, Soapy continued his trance-like stare across the bar.

Then as he continued to staring blankly he called out, "Sheeny." The Sheeny Kid answered right away with "Yes Mr. Smith?" Soapy continued, but he never turned to look at the men. "I want you to go and keep a sharp eye on that group that was just here. Report back to me the moment you learn anything." The Sheeny Kid was excited but nervous that he'd been given orders from Soapy as he quickly said, "Yes sir" and headed for the door.

Soapy continued staring across the bar as he added, "Sheeny." The Sheeny Kid stopped abruptly and turned around to look at Soapy. But there was nothing but uncomfortable silence. Then in a low voice, Soapy said, "Be careful." Surprised and somewhat dismayed, the Sheeny Kid answered in an equally low voice, "Yes sir."

The Raging Storm Had Arrived

An angry crowd had gathered at the town meeting place called Sylvester Hall.

Everyone agreed on one thing. They were going to run Soapy Smith and his gang out of Skagway. Inside the hall it was noisy and standing room only as Ed Williams pushed his way inside. By the time the Sheeny Kid had arrived at the hall to keep an eye on things for Soapy, it was too crowded inside so Sheeny pushed his way to the open door so he could at least stand there and listen to what was going on.

First, the Commissioner stood up in front and settled down the crowd so they could start the meeting. "Friends, we have to put an end to this scoundrel's activities here in Skagway." The people in the hall erupted. They cheered, stamped there feet and hollered in loud approval. Then the Commissioner motioned for the crowd to settle back down as he continued. "It's not just Mr. Stewart's gold. That was only the final straw. This man Smith has given Skagway a bad name. And his cons, thievery and strong-arm tactics have driven off a good number of decent folks. I believe that we must all band together on this night and run Smith and his men out of Skagway." Again, the hall erupted with loud cheers.

Just outside the hall, a man named Tom Baker recognized the Sheeny Kid as one of Soapy's men and asked, "Say, ain't you one of Soapy's boys?" Another man named Jed Forester turned to look and also recognized Sheeny. "I believe he is one a them." Then Tom Baker moved in close to a nervous Sheeny and said, "If you know what's good for ya, you'll go back to Smith and tell him to git." Sheeny gladly took their advice and quickly left. Tom Baker and Jed Forester watched as The Sheeny Kid scurried down the street.

It's Eight O'Clock Smith - Get Out

Inside the Parlor, Soapy was still at the bar, not facing his men as they continued to wait it out. Suddenly, the Sheeny Kid rushed in out of breath as he blurted, "It ain't good Mr. Smith. There talking about running you clean out of town." A concerned Reverend Bowers spoke up in a strong voice and tried to assure Soapy and the men by saying, "It's talk, just talk." The Parlor was silent. Then Soapy turned around quickly to face his men and said, "So that's it. They think they can push us around. Well boys, we still have a few aces up our sleeves."

Suddenly, from outside the Parlor, the Commissioner called for Soapy. "Smith, it's eight o'clock." But there was no response from inside the Parlor. After a few more moments of silence, Frank Reid hollered from the street. "Smith, we're waiting."

Outside, a crowd from Sylvester Hall had gathered to confront Soapy and his men.

Inside the Parlor, Soapy headed for the door as a concerned Ed Burns followed close behind.

Outside, the front door swung open and Smith appeared in the doorway and defiantly looked out at the murmuring, torch-bearing crowd. Seeing Soapy, the crowd settled down, waiting to hear what he had to say. Ed

Williams stood there in the crowd too, and asked himself, "What's this Smith fella going to do?" In a moment, he would find out.

Smith looked the crowd over and defiantly stated, "I told you before, Stewart lost his gold in a fair game of cards and that's an end to it." Then Frank Reid spoke up loudly with, "You're a liar Smith." The crowd shouted in agreement. Quickly, Soapy hollered back, "And you're a pack of fools!" And with that, Smith stepped back into the Parlor and slammed the door shut.

From the crowd outside, a man named Murphy shouted, "lets go get him." But Major Strong said, "No! I say we meet down at the Juneau Wharf and set our plans to run Smith and his gang out of town."

The Commissioner jumped in with, "I agree. Let's get moving so we can put an end to this thing once and for all." Then the torch-bearing crowd followed the Commissioner, Major Strong and Frank Reid to Juneau Wharf.

Back inside the Parlor, Soapy's men didn't know what to say. Then, Reverend Bowers spoke up. "What if we give back the gold?" Soapy quickly looked at the Reverend and said, "Because if we do that... we're through."

Doc Jackson offered, "But it doesn't look good now boss. I think maybe..." A suddenly furious, Soapy cut him off by shouting, "No! I do the thinking around here!" Soapy angrily kicked a chair across the room, and it barely missed some of his men.

This Could Get Ugly

Major Strong told the torch bearing crowd to stop at the entrance to Juneau Wharf.

Strong said, "I think we should post a guard here at the entrance to the wharf. That way, we can keep Smith and his men from interfering with our meeting." The Commissioner agreed. Then Frank Reid stepped forward and offered, "I'll stand guard here. I know Smith and most of his men. Some of you fellas with torches stay here too so I'll have some light."

A moment later, errie shadows danced as torches on either side of Frank Reid provided at least some light as he stood guard over the entrance. The rest of the crowd had moved on down to the other end of the wharf. As Frank Reid stood there, he thought about what would happen if Soapy and his men showed up. The night air was filled with danger.

I'll Show em

Still inside Jeff Smith's Parlor, Soapy looked at his bartender, Nate Pollock and sternly commanded, "Nate, give me my rifle."

As Nate quickly did as he was told, Reverend Bowers and the others tensed up. Again the Parlor was deadly quiet. After a moment, Bowers broke the silence. "What's your plan brother Jefferson?" Soapy took his rifle from Nate, then looked at Bowers. "I'm going to show Skagway just who Jefferson Randolph Smith is." And with that, an angry Soapy headed for the door with great resolve. Ed Burns followed close behind. Reverend Bowers, Doc Jackson, George Wilder, the Sheeny Kid and several others followed.

Out on the muddy street, Soapy and his men headed for Juneau Wharf.

As he walked down the street, Soapy waved his rifle and snarled at passers by, "Chase yourselves to bed." Then as he rounded the corner to Juneau Wharf, Soapy spotted a shadowy figure of a man at the entrance, standing between two torch-bearing figures. Soapy stopped suddenly, then turned toward his men and told them, "That's far enough. I go the rest of the way by myself. And that includes you Ed." Reverend Bowers became concerned and protested. "Brother Jefferson. I fear this is not a wise move." Soapy then looked at the Reverend as his men waited in silence. After a quiet moment, Soapy turned away from his men and looked ahead at Juneau Wharf. The silence was deafening. Then sure and determined, Soapy walked strong and proud toward the shadowy figure of a man at the entrance to the wharf.

You Can't Come Down Here Smith

As Soapy approached, the shadowy figure of a man called out. "Smith, you can't come down here."

Soapy was holding his rifle low by his side, as he continued to walk straight up to the shadowy figure he knew was Frank Reid. Confident he could push past Reid, Soapy stopped right in front of him and figured to bully his way to the other end of the wharf. As the two stood face-to-face, the only sound was the flickering windswept flames of the two torches.

Soapy spoke first with, "Reid, you're at the bottom of this. I should have gotten rid of you months ago."

And with that, the world went into a terrifying slow motion.

Soapy swung the barrel of his rifle up hard against the left side of Reid's head. Reid flinched in pain as his head jolted to the right. To defend himself, Reid quickly reacted as he grabbed Soapy's rifle barrel with his left hand and swiftly pushed it down and away.

That was as far as Soapy thought it would go. He thought Reid would step aside.

But a wide-eyed Reid was afraid because he thought Soapy was going to kill him. So Reid quickly moved his right hand to his revolver and jerked it from it's holster.

Both men knew they were in a life or death struggle. To them, there was no time in the world. There was no sound. Only the strange sense of darkness and death that would come at the hands of the other.

Nervous and breathing hard, Reid pointed his quivering gun filled hand right at Soapy. Somehow, Reid pulled the trigger of his revolver. The snapping sound of the hammer as it slammed against the bullet in the chamber was all the two heard. It was clear. One of them was going to die.

But the round in the chamber of Frank Reid's revolver was a dud and didn't fire. Then Soapy feverishly tried to stop what was about to happen, as he shouted, "No Reid!" But it was too late.

Soapy feared for his life and in a world of slow motion, Soapy swung his rifle barrel up, but pulled the trigger early. Orange flame shot from his rifle barrel and the bullet slammed deep into Reid's groin. At the same time Soapy had fired his rifle, Reid pulled the trigger on his gun a second time. His revolver was fired point blank. The bullet ripped through Soapy's chest and tore through his heart.

Soapy was blown backwards. Reid fell at the same time, but he somehow managed to get off two more shots. Both struck Soapy.

It was over.

All that was left was the night air filled with the smell of smoke from the quick blast of their guns and the crackling sound of the torch lights. Soapy's men stood there in the dark, frozen in time and horrified by what they had just witnessed.

Eerie Shadows Dance

Ed Williams and the rest of the crowd at the far end of the wharf had turned quickly to look in the direction of the gun shots, just in time to see Soapy and Reid fall backwards onto the wharf. Then Ed Williams and the crowd rushed back to the entrance of the wharf to find out what happened. Ed's knees wobbled as he tried to keep up.

When Ed got there, he was breathing hard and his entire body was shaking as he looked down at the two men sprawled out on their backs at his feet.

The men with the torches who had stayed with Reid had bent down over him. Reid had been wounded badly and had bled all over the wharf. The gathered crowd was out of breath and shook as the two torch bearers told the crowd what happened. They kept repeating, "It happened so fast! It happened so fast!"

The bloody hole in Soapy's chest told the story. Soapy was dead before he hit the wharf. As Ed Williams looked down, the flickering light made strange, eerie shadows that danced on Soapy's dead body. Ed's heart pounded. He could not stop shaking and he could not speak. He could scarcely believe what he had seen. Ed Williams would never forget this horrible night.

It was all much more than he had bargained for.

Soapy's Last Bluff

The next day, the Skaguay News carried the following front page headline.

"Soapy Smith's Last Bluff Called by Frank Reid." Then it read, "Armed With a Winchester, He Endeavors to Intimidate a Large Meeting of Indignant Citizens on the Third Wharf."

For Ed Williams, the newspaper had called it right and true. Twelve days later, Frank Reid died from his wound. A funeral was held for him in a church Soapy had helped to build. A large marble monument had been erected over Frank Reid's grave with the following inscription. "He gave his life for the honor of Skagway."

Soapy Smith was buried outside the cemetery so as not to "Desecrate the hollowed ground."

All Different

It had all been exhausting.

Ed Williams had been there at Sylvester Hall, then out side of Jeff Smith's Parlor and later at Juneau Wharf. And he was there moments after the gunfight.

As he walked the ever muddy streets of Skagway, except for the talk on the street and rounding up Soapy's men to run them out of town, it was still Skagway.

As Ed looked around, he suddenly realized that Gold Fever had left him. Or maybe he had left it the last time he found a filthy coin while he cleaned out a spittoon in Clancy's Saloon.

It was going to be different. Soapy was gone. But how much different? They wouldn't find all the con men and thugs. Some would still be in town. And stampeders would still have to make the hard trip up the Chilkoot Pass and the White Pass before they could even start to make their way to the gold fields. Sure, some guy named George Carmack struck it rich and others had as well. But Ed Williams didn't want to end up like J.D. Stewart. Ed didn't want to be so taken with Gold Fever that he'd let himself get half frozen while he kept digging with his last ounce of strength for a smidgen of gold dust in some frozen hard creek bed.

So Ed made plans to stick around just long enough to buy a ticket for a stream ship that would take him back home.

One thing was sure. His journey to Skagway and his time there was going to be something his children and grandchildren would be hearing about.

And what about all that gold? Ed thought to himself. His answer was, "Well, you can show them the coin. You don't have to tell them that you had actually found the coin in that spittoon in Clancy's. You can tell them the coin had come from your gold strike. Of course it had come from a gold strike... just not yours. But nobody had to know where that coin really came from. Well, maybe you could tell a person or two. Yeah, that would work."

Where Did You Strike Gold?

A couple of days later.

Ed Williams stood on the deck of a steamship, holding on to the railing as he watched Skagway get smaller on the horizon as his ship made it's way out of the wind and mist of Skagway Bay.

Then a man walked up beside Ed, took hold of the wet railing, looked at him and asked, "Did you strike gold?" Ed looked at the man and thought about his answer. Impatient, the man asked again, "Well, did you?" Ed continued to look at the man as he said, "Yeah... yeah I did." The man looked interested and pressed Ed with, "Where?" A sly grin crossed Ed's face and he proudly answered, "In the bottom of a spittoon in Clancy's Saloon." The man was surprised, furrowed his brow and gave Ed a puzzled look.

Pleased with himself, Ed turn, smiled and walked away. And as he walked across the deck, he remember that darned headline. "GOLD! GOLD! GOLD! GOLD! Sixty-Eight Rich Men on the Steamer Portland. STACKS OF YELLOW METAL!

The End

About the Author

Michael R Dougherty authored this book about the gold rush and Soapy Smith, but you can call him Mike.

Mike first moved to Alaska from California when he was just 3 years old. He took his parents with him.

Research for a motion picture screenplay about Soapy Smith led to an interest in the Alaska Gold Rush of 1897 to 1898. It was a fascinating event in history.

Some years ago, Mike got to meet Jeff Smith, the great-grandson of Jefferson Randolph "Soapy" Smith. For Mike, it was like getting to meet Soapy himself.

Mike used to write with pencils. His wife sharpened them. She used a steak knife. Now, Mike writes with a compute. Mike misses writing with a pencil and he misses watching his wife sharpen them with a steak knife.